GW01043924

MISS BROWNE'S FRIEND

ZEPHYR BOOKS

Classic short works

MISS BROWNE'S FRIEND

A STORY OF TWO WOMEN

by

F. M. MAYOR

Zephyr Books

SANDNESS
MICHAEL WALMER
2021

Miss Browne's Friend first published serially June 1914 to March 1915
in the *Free Church Suffrage Times*

This edition published 2021

by

Michael Walmer
North House
Melby
Sandness
Shetland ZE2 9PL

ISBN 978-0-6489204-5-8 hardcover

CHAPTER I

IN almost every village in England a Miss Browne is to be found; in every town several Miss Brownes; in London they must be almost too many to count. We all know them, spinsters from thirty onwards, who are cheerfully devoting their lives to be of use and comfort to their families, their friends, their village, their town, and their country. Sometimes these objects of their goodness patronize them, sometimes they laugh at them, and sometimes they writhe a little under the benefits they are receiving; but they could not possibly get on without their Miss Brownes.

This Miss Browne lived at Croydon, and waited on a mother who did not want waiting on, was at the beck and call of two brothers, their wives, and children, and kept all responsibilities from a younger sister who went to the Slade, and employed herself in painting what her mother, with the candid tongue of the older generation, described as "disgusting things of naked Italians." Miss Browne was, in short, of the valuable type which is patronized.

She long remembered the day when she read an article in a little magazine, the organ of a philanthropic society, urging ladies to befriend the girls who were trained in its Rescue Home. "They are so solitary, poor lassies," said the article, with that bright pathos which is the special property of philanthropic magazines, "not a soul to care for them. Who will take them by the hand?"

In consequence of this appeal, Miss Browne was appointed "friend" to Mabel Roberts, and after an exchange of letters she found herself one March afternoon bumped up and down in a motor-bus on her way to visit her *protégée* at the Rescue Home.

A Sister in nurse's dress greeted her: a Sister who somehow put one in mind of angels, although one surmises that angels are as a rule radiant and victorious, and this little Sister was tottering not very far from the brink of a nervous breakdown. Yet there was something important, though intangible, which she shared with them, and which actually, when one saw her and Miss Browne

2

together, made her, a woman born and bred in the working classes, reduce refined, cultivated Miss Browne, with generations of gentility behind her, not merely to utter mediocrity, but almost to vulgarity.

Miss Browne was conducted through rooms containing numbers of girls in blue print dresses and large aprons. It came as a shock to her that, on the whole, they were not fascinating, not handsome, not pretty, not even passably nice looking. Most of them had fat, red cheeks, and an expression of stolid cheerfulness on their faces. But one in the sewing-room was different. Her small, lithe figure, drooping neck, and eyes of a piercing blue might have belonged to the poetic daughter of an earl. She looked at Miss Browne as they passed, and the loveliest blush swept across her face. "I do hope she's Mabel," thought Miss Browne. Possessing a face which no one (herself included) could ever remember much about, she had a peculiar tenderness for beauty. They came back to the little waiting-room, an ugly little room, but one could not help being drawn to it, when one thought of the many strange and touching histories it might have related, could it have spoken, of what had been enacted within its walls.

"I'll send Mabel," said Sister, "she's so looking forward to seeing you."

Miss Browne had a minute to study the castor-oil plant and "The Lord is My Light," in silver letters on a crimson ground, and to crush two thoughts which had assailed her already several times on her way. One, the dislike of coming in contact with anything which was depraved; other, a kind of envy underneath the shrinking. Mabel had had the experience which every woman has the right to claim from life, and she had never had it: a man had desired her.

The door opened, and the beauty of the sewing-room entered. Miss Browne felt so shy, not from repulsion, but from awe at the loveliness before her, that for a minute she could not speak, only give the violets she had brought with a timid "I thought you might...."

"Oh, miss, violets, the flowers I love more than any others. I shall give some to Florrie, she's my great friend. It's her collar I'm wearing, miss. Her sister gave it to her, but she says to me 'You must have it for your lady friend.'"

The vision found no difficulty in talking, and made Miss Browne feel that even in this little half-hour they had come close to intimacy.

4

"Yes, there's something very attractive about Mabel," said Sister, as she let Miss Browne out, "and we hope great things, if you will befriend her. We have not been able," her mild, almost, too sensitive face frowning in earnestness, "to bring out what is best in her. I feel sure there must be something hidden away."

All the way home Miss Browne thought of Mabel's parting words: "I didn't seem to want to try hard before, but now I have a friend who cares for me I mean to do my very best," and she almost forgot to get out at her proper turning, she was so busy with benevolent schemes for Mabel's future.

The next visit to the Home Mabel seemed almost more charming, a certain wanness adding an irresistible pathos. She had crocheted a doyley for Miss Browne, and said "Will you ask Sister if you may speak to Florrie? Florrie reads your letters, and she does envy me." Florrie, a wizened looking girl with glasses, whom it was difficult to realize had had charms sufficient to tempt any man, had no gift of polite conversation, and her voice, when she allowed it to be heard, was gruff.

Sister looked more wan than Mabel. "Things have been rather difficult with her lately," said she. "I haven't been patient enough. I think it may be better when she gets away. If one only knew a little more where one was with her. Florrie? Oh yes, Florrie's a little Trojan, you can trust Florrie anywhere."

A few days after Miss Browne received one of Mabel's letters. They had a simplicity which was so exactly suited to the writer that one might have thought an author, a good author, had composed them:-

MY OWN DEAR MISS BROWNE,

I hardly like to tell you, but I must, for I cannot bear to keep *anything* from you. I was very rude to Sister yesterday morning. I said a dreadful thing to her, and she said she would write and tell you, and oh I feel so miserable. I went away and cried, and then I prayed to God and asked Him to forgive me, and I have asked Sister and she says she will, and now can you, dear Miss Browne, for if you do not, I do not know *what* I shall do.

Your poor

MABEL.

No one was more modest than Miss Browne, but she could not help wondering why Sister found Mabel difficult.

And now Mabel was to go to a place, and Miss Browne out of her small store helped to provide the outfit. She allowed herself one treat in the year, a walking tour with her dearly loved brother. It was a wrench to part with her stout, strong boots, yet she had a sentimental pleasure in giving them to Mabel. She had in her life the happiness of being quite indispensable, but she was rather taken for granted. "My own dear Miss Browne" gave her more pleasure than she realized, and she would have been ashamed to own how much she was under the power of those large eyes.

Mabel was established as general with two elderly ladies, humbler and older types of the *genus* Browne. Glowing letters constantly came. "Miss Bretherton has given me a hat, and yesterday there were some oranges, and she said I might finish them, and Miss Ellen has given me two post cards of Ilfracombe; isn't that kind of them? I mean to try my very best, because they are so very kind, and that will please you I know." This sounded very well. Florrie, also at a place, came to tea to meet Mabel, and the affection of the two girls for one another, their devotion to Miss Browne, and their delight in her collection of Italian post cards made a pretty little scene, worthy of an old-fashioned Sunday story-book.

Happy letters continued to arrive. Miss Browne was just reading the latest, when the afternoon post came in, bringing with it a less happy communication from Mabel's mistress. Half a page of politeness, and then, "Mabel has not been going on *at all* satisfactorily. She has been most impertinent about the *dog,* and we find that she does *not* go to church in the evening, as she is supposed to do, but walks about the streets! As she has no relations, and seems so poor, we are unwilling to send her away. She wears *very* thin stockings for the time of year, and goes out in house shoes with high heels! And she says she cannot afford to buy anything stronger." In the light of this, Miss Browne read Mabel's letter for the third time. "I love going to church, dear Miss Browne; we sing that pretty hymn you say you like, 'O Jesus, I have promised,' and I always think of you. Your own Mabel." The whole taste had gone out of Miss Browne's tea, and she almost forgot to answer her mother cheerfully.

That evening Florrie came to call. She could hardly find adequate words to speak of Mabel's baseness. "Oh, and those boots you gave her. 'Me wear them,' she says, 'do well enough for a freak like her,' she says, 'but I'm not a blooming suffragette,' that's what she said about you, Miss Browne (Mabel used this term, it is to be feared, as one of extreme reproach), and she went and pawned them, and I'm never going to speak to her again."

After many hours of lying awake, Miss Browne forced herself to go and see Mabel. A glance at her little, lovely ankle made it evident that she should never have been expected to wear walking boots. There was a tender scene, and "I promise you I will *always* tell you everything." Her mistresses, kind and prim people, were persuaded into giving her another chance. Soon a letter from Florrie. "Me and Mabel had such a nice walk last Sunday, she says she would rather go about with me than with boys, so we are always going out together Sundays before evening church, and she has given me two lovely post cards, because she says I have not got so many as her." Rather startling, but most satisfactory.

CHAPTER II

BY the end of four months Mabel had left her place. "And I daresay it's a good thing," thought Miss Browne; "they didn't make sufficient allowance. She will do better this time."

This was also Mabel's view. "I shall do better this time, I know. My mistress is so very kind, and she says I'm such a comical girl—I make her laugh. I mean to do my very, very best."

Enthusiastic letters from mistress and maid for a month or so, then silence; then a letter with a sad resemblance to Miss Bretherton's. "She is very rude, and her temper is quite unbearable. I cannot possibly keep her."

By the same post came an aggrieved letter from Mabel. "I could not stay here, even if you wished me. It is a Boarding House, and some of the people are very American in their ways. Dear Miss Browne, it is not a house you would like me to be in, and it is an untruth to say I hit anybody. I may have just touched Mrs. Burrows with my elbow by accident, but that is all." She left.

"Perhaps it is a good thing," thought Miss Browne; "Mrs. Burrows is a rough, common woman. She has hardly the tact to manage Mabel. Things will be better this time."

Eighteen months after the beginning of the friendship Mabel started in her seventh place, as general to Mrs. Marks at a new suburb beyond Hendon. She was in the middle of her fourth quarrel with Florrie; at present they were not on speaking terms.

The usual letter announced: "There are three little children, and the eldest is called Ethel, so I love her best of all, because that is your name. I am dressing them some dolls. My mistress says she has never had a girl iron table-cloths as smooth as me. Isn't that nice? I am sure I shall like being here, and I mean to try *very* hard, so that you can be proud of your Mabel."

Miss Browne knew that sentence too well, and was beginning to hate it. She also knew rather too well the first enthusiastic letter of the mistress.

12

"Mabel is such a willing girl, and such an excellent worker. I shall make allowances for her temper, for I have got one myself."

After the first six weeks of constant correspondence, Miss Browne began to dread the letters, or rather the absence of letters. For ten days there was complete silence, then Mabel wrote: "I am so miserable, and I am going out to drown myself. This is the last letter you will ever get from your broken-hearted Mabel."

It was a grilling day—July at its most odious; and no one is expected to travel from Croydon to a new suburb beyond Hendon in the space of anything so short as a morning. "Delamere," Waterloo Avenue, seemed quite unknown to all the inhabitants, and Miss Browne tramped over tracts of unfinished streets of villas before, at last, she knocked at its highly ornamented door.

Mrs. Marks opened it.

"Where is Mabel?" said Miss Browne, almost too tired to articulate even that short phrase coherently.

"Sitting in the kitchen, and won't do a thing. She's been like it for three days, and I can't get a char, or I'd turn her straight out of the house. I'm afraid for the children to go near her."

"Oh, I'm so thankful," said Miss Browne, half sobbing; "she told me she was going to drown herself."

"Tcha!" said Mrs. Marks.

Then Miss Browne was taken into the drawing-room, and a long soliloquy was delivered by Mrs. Marks. First about servants, this girl and that; how depraved they were, and how weakly, absurdly kind she was. Then the topic changed, and Miss Browne in a whirl of fatigue could distinguish over and over again such phrases as "awfully smart restaurant," "frightfully expensive," and "his own racing car." At last she was allowed to go into the kitchen, and there she saw the most dismal spectacle. She would not have recognized the smart, radiant Mabel in the creature that sat huddled in a chair. What she said to it she did not know. She scolded, implored, caressed, and Mabel never answered a word. She had sometimes fancied that Mabel's tempers were figments of mistresses; now she knew better.

In the evening Florrie, who had stayed steadily in one place—she and her mistress contenting themselves with mutual grumbles—came to plead for Mabel. "Do, please, forgive her; she says you are the only person that ever cared for her, and now you don't. Miss Browne, I shall never be happy again if you don't forgive her."

The next day came a letter from Mrs. Marks. "Mabel has apologized, so I think she may as well stay on, as my husband says she has such a good appearance; and my little girl was taken ill last night, and she's really very useful in sitting up with her." So apparently mistresses can be quick-change artists too.

That peace was not patched up for long, however, and after the next outburst Miss Browne felt that service had been given a sufficient chance, and that it was time to try something else. Mabel became a waitress, and in the greater latitude of adornment now permitted, no French actress, with all the resources of art and intelligence at her command, could have arranged her hair more bewitchingly right than Mabel.

Everything went beautifully—until the usual earthquake.

"Miss Browne," said Florrie, "I wish you'd speak to Mabel about that fellow. I don't mean the chap she was about with all last year; he was bad enough, but this one's a lot worse. I've spoken so often, and she would care if you said something."

Miss Browne had often thought to comfort herself, when she needed comfort: "At any rate, she has certainly given up the old life. I don't think Mabel ever sees, or wishes to see, a man at all."

What that life had been before the Rescue Home Miss Browne had never inquired, nor had she and Mabel ever referred to love or marriage. Once Mabel had said with that endearing smile, which still had power, though less power than formerly, to stir Miss Browne: "She sent me a post-card I didn't like, which you wouldn't have liked either, so I threw it into the fire." Otherwise her views on such subjects were a closed book. In fact, as Miss Browne sometimes reflected, almost all her views were a closed book. She began to recognize that what had first seemed such transparent candour concealed a reserve difficult to penetrate. She knew little more of Mabel's inner self than the first day she had seen her.

Miss Browne found the subject very difficult to approach with Mabel, and walked shyly round and round it, as it were. At last it got as near as "I am afraid there is some one—you know some one— you are going about with some one—"

"Me, Miss Browne?"

"Yes, I think there is a man whom your mother would not like."

"She—oh, she never cared—as long as we kept out of her way."

"Then we care, dear. There are dangers—I mean—you know, it isn't always safe—"

"Oh no, miss," said Mabel, opening her innocent eyes; "some girls are so silly."

CHAPTER III

THEN the news came that Mabel had been dismissed from the Restaurant. Miss Browne, who was getting to know much of London and its environs from journeys to interview Mabel's employers, went to plead with the manager.

"Well, madam," said he, "since you ask me—it was her behaviour with customers. Of course, this is a superior place, where we cater for ladies and family parties after *matinées* and such, and we have to be particular. What the girls do outside is no concern of ours. I shouldn't be surprised if some of them added to their wages now and then; we don't expect they live on what we give them. But we must have correct behaviour in business hours. Ladies were complaining."

Miss Browne's face must have shown something of what she was feeling, for he went on: "You know, madam, you really cannot judge these girls as we should do ourselves; they're not like one of us."

"I hope they're not," said she.

It was just the answer she did not mean to make; but she was easily talked down and bewildered by men, particularly by one so stout, noisy, and prosperous.

"I really think," said her mother on her return, "it's a waste of time trapesing after that girl, and in the rain, too. Besides, it doesn't seem to me quite what one likes—and when there are so many excellent societies just for that purpose."

"And it's so foolish, Ethel, because those girls like that sort of life."

This consolation came from her younger sister, who was just as ignorant as girls of twenty-two in the protected classes have always been, but was so pathetically anxious not to be Victorian.

It seemed that Mabel had cut herself off from everyone. Florrie, the faithful medium of communication when things went wrong, this time knew nothing. She could only surmise that "that nasty Lena"—Miss Browne had never heard of

Lena's existence—"had got hold of her again. She's always been after her."

Apparently, then, the Mabel episode was over—gone, dead, and gradually to be forgotten. But for weeks Miss Browne found herself standing at street corners, looking for the impossible chance that, among all the numberless passing girls of London, one should be Mabel. And one actually was. She was arm in arm with a coarse, rather handsome young woman. She saw Miss Browne, and first turned scarlet through her powder, and then white. She wanted to escape, but Miss Browne was too quick for her.

"Mabel, I've been thinking of you so often, and wondering where you were."

"Have you, Miss?" said Mabel. Miss Browne had never seen her embarrassed before. "Didn't you get my letter?"

Neither of them believed in the letter, however. "Won't you come and have tea with me now, you and your friend?"

"All right," said Lena, "I don't mind."

They went into an A B C shop, empty at that moment—the rush of tea customers was over; and for years after an A B C shop brought the strangest scene back to Miss Browne. Here was the opportunity so long waited for, and now it had come how unutterably she wished it had not. It could not be of long duration, but in her state of tension each minute dragged interminably, but though interminable each brought her nearer to that dreadful instant of time when she must speak to Mabel. Her flesh and her spirit, both equally weak, shrank away from it, and she had a kind of nightmare horror that Lena might do something to her—she did not know what—strike her or attack her. Lena and Mabel were nervous, too. Lena in her nervousness was inclined to be uproarious. They had both been drinking a little, and one could hear Mabel panting. Conversation of some sort was maintained, but neither girl could stay long at any topic. Lena's contributions were confined for the most part to comments on the advertisements surrounding them. "That's all right, isn't it?" or "That's silly," and then loud laughter. None of the three could bear to be silent. At the time Miss Browne did not seem to take in what was being talked about, but afterwards she recollected that Mabel had said she and Lena were living together, and took in sewing, and were getting on nicely, thank you. It wasn't such hard work as the restaurant, and some of the girls there were so fast—she had been glad to leave.

Suddenly it struck half-past six. Miss Browne was dining early, and going to the theatre that night. The appeal must be made at once. She had been composing the beginnings of numberless sentences, but her brain had not been steady enough to finish one of them.

"Mabel, I want you to find another place in a restaurant, will you?"

"Me, Miss Browne? but I'm getting on so nicely with the sewing."

"Yes, but I know such a nice place out of London where you could live; it would be so much healthier."

"I think London suits me best, Miss Browne. It's so damp anywhere out of London."

She gave up trying to be diplomatic.

"I want you to leave this life, Mabel. Do, do, *do* give it up, dear. Lena, *don't* persuade her to stay!"

"Oh, I shan't say anything," said Lena, all kindness, and not making herself in the least disagreeable; "she can do what she likes, for me."

At these last two speeches, particularly at Miss Browne's (she had no idea, how loud she was talking), the manageress and waitresses, already keenly interested, were excited to fever pitch, and made up errands of carrying about teacups to adjoining tables, so that they should not miss one word.

Mabel looked away, and did not answer. Then suddenly, when Miss Browne had put her hand imploringly on her shoulder, she turned round, her eyes swimming in tears, and said, "I don't mind if I do give it up; I'm not so happy if it comes to that."

Time was so short that Miss Browne could not do more than write down Mabel's address, and arrange to fetch her and her possessions in a cab at three o'clock the next day.

It had been wonderfully easy. Yes, certainly, it is true

....the clouds we so much dread

Are big with mercy, and shall break

In blessings on our head.

CHAPTER IV

NEXT morning, Miss Browne went to an old servant, a widow, who lived alone, and arranged that Mabel should board with her. She went also to the laundry they employed, and appealed to the manageress to take Mabel. Everyone was sympathetic and anxious to help, and all was satisfactorily arranged, down to the bunch of violets in memory of their first meeting, which she put to welcome Mabel on the mantlepiece.

At three o'clock she knocked at the door of a quiet house in a small street. It was opened by a very fat woman, exactly, as it immediately struck Miss Browne, what Lena would be, if she lived ten years longer.

"Does Mabel Roberts live here?"

"She did, madam," said the woman primly, as if on her very best behaviour, "but she left this morning."

"She *left*. But I said I shouldn't come till three. Where has she gone, do you know?"

"That I really cannot say, madam. They would not leave any address."

"Could I see Lena, then?"

"Her friend Lena went with her."

"And her boxes?"

"They took the boxes with them."

It was a few moments before Miss Browne could take in that all her hopes had crumbled away, then she turned upon the woman.

"Oh, *why* didn't you let her come with me? *Why* didn't you let her have a chance?"

"Well, I do call that good," said the woman, changing suddenly into her natural self, "wantin' to force the pore girl into a Home, and takin' the bread out of her mouth, and then blamin' me. She never meant to go, of course, and it wouldn't have been a bit of good if you'd got her. I know you ladies who tries and gets them into Homes, but they *always comes back*. Wasn't your name Browne? They did have a hearty laugh about you last night, I can tell you."

All there was to be done now was to get into the cab and drive home.

Her relations were most kind. Her mother did not say, "Well, I always thought it was rather a mistake, but I did not wish to discourage you," more than three times; and her sister said nothing at all, being so busy with high artistic pursuits, that she had forgotten weeks ago that there had ever been such a person as Mabel Roberts. And it was well they were kind, for at first the disappointment was anguish. Gradually she became inured to it.

For another interval of several months Miss Browne heard nothing of Mabel. And now she was not always watching for her. She had tried and tried, and hoped against hope, and it had been in vain; she had not even been able to make Mabel care for her.

At last it was again Florrie who wrote, "Mabel is in the infirmary and she does want to see you; but she says she knows you won't forgive her, but I said I would ask you. I think she looks very bad."

She went to see Mabel. Sister (poles apart from the angelic Sister) was so much occupied with some breach of etiquette of which Miss Browne had been guilty, that she had hardly time to answer questions. "Oh, yes, Mabel Roberts. She's a very tiresome patient, making mischief with all the others, and one can't believe a word she says—most *trying.*"

It is probable that no one but Mabel could have succeeded in being smart in the dressing jacket of a workhouse infirmary; but though still smart, she looked very ill, and indescribably altered. She was delighted to see Miss Browne, and showed her, with all her old charm, a picture postcard of a rosy, vivacious lady, carrying a dog, with the remark, "I always love that card, because I think she's like you." Neither referred at all to the past. The conversation was a little feverish, on safe topics, such as the intelligence of fox-terriers, the beauty of a spring day, and a pretty story—Mabel could always tell pretty stories—of little Evie in the next bed, who had been crying because her dolly had no warm frock now the weather was cold, and how Mabel had made one for her. But Miss Browne could not help feeling that all this was Mabel's wonderfully skilful method of extracting 5s.; 5s. she had so foolishly given again and again in the past.

She was kind, for such was her nature that she never could be anything but kind, but in her heart she felt repulsion to Mabel. When the time came to go, she remembered her utter loneliness, and kissed her, but she was glad when the kiss was done. She turned to look back at the door, and she saw a blush of perfect joy spread itself all over Mabel's face. "How *can* she do it?" she thought. Sister had recovered her equanimity, and was ready for a word or two in the corridor, that spotless, dreadful corridor, stretching out to infinity. "No, doctor doesn't think it will be immediate, but she can't get better," and then she said with an earnestness, which made Miss Browne feel that after all she did not only care about having a more perfectly put on cap than any one in England, "Why should one hope she should? What *is* there for her when she goes out?"

A few days after, Miss Browne, surrounded by her nieces and nephews, was in the middle of a delicious game of "Follow my leader." A commercial-looking envelope was handed to her, and when she opened it, she found a printed form, compiled with such elaborate efforts at simplification for mean capacities that she had to read it three times before she could come to any conclusion. Then it appeared that Mabel Roberts was dead (Nature having disagreed with the doctor), and that as she had no relations, Miss Browne was requested forthwith to come and take charge of her possessions.

Burning was the only destiny for her poor, tattered openwork stockings, lacy petticoat, transparent blouse, and underclothes all over dirty bows, for apparently temper goes against one also in that profession; but there was a box of treasures which Miss Browne examined. She found some Christmas cards, photographs of Mabel, of herself, of Lena, and of various men, a half-finished doyley which, judging from the seven already presented to her, Miss Browne rightly surmised was a Christmas gift for her, two objectionable postcards sent, as a little calculation would have enabled her to discover, about the date when Mabel had made her pious declaration concerning postcards, a pretty booklet with a verse, whose poetry was not quite up to its sentiment, one of those verses composed, one imagines, by gentle elderly ladies, confined to their sofas, or, perhaps, one is wrong, and on the contrary, they are tossed off in hundreds by astute young men.

But the bulkiest part of the treasure was every one of her letters and postcards, and every one of her envelopes. This touched Miss Browne even more, because she did not realize the strange passion of the poor for envelopes.

Florrie came to tea soon afterwards to talk about Mabel. She cried a very great deal, and when she could speak, she began that eulogy of the dead which poor people are so particularly generous in bestowing, such a eulogy that no one would have guessed there had ever been a cloud between the two.

"Miss Browne, she *did* try, Mabel did. Once we was going along Edgware Road, Mabel and me, and that fellow Davies she was so fond of, came out of a public, and he said, 'Come and have a drink,' and she says, 'No,' and he says, 'You shall,' and she says, 'No, I shan't,' and he says, 'Well, I'll make you,' and he dragged her arm awful, and made her scream, and he made her go in, and he gave her some beer, Miss Browne, and she threw it on the floor, and she fought her way out, she did give him one in the eye, and she says to me, 'Run as hard as we can, or I know I shall yield,' and I says, 'Why don't you have a glass, Mabel?' and she says, 'Because I know the Treasure'—that's what her and me always called you, Miss Browne— 'wouldn't like it.' "

"She said that?" said Miss Browne, shakily, "I had no idea."

When it was time for Florrie to go, Miss Browne kissed her so tenderly, that Florrie could hardly believe her happiness. She did not know that half that kiss, or perhaps all of it, was meant for Mabel; that Miss Browne longed more than she could say that somehow or other, wherever Mabel was, even if, which was so hard to imagine, she was now a glorious spirit in bliss, beyond all mortal cares, that kiss of love might reach her.